79375
Parrots Don't Make House Calls

Trina Wiebe
AR B.L.: 4.0
Points: 2.0   LG

Parrots Don't Make House Calls

by Trina Wiebe

Illustrations
by Marisol Sarrazin

Lobster Press™

To all the wonderful kids and teachers
at Kelly Creek Community School.

Parrots Don't Make House Calls
Text © 2003 Trina Wiebe
Illustrations © 2003 Marisol Sarrazin

Published in 2007 by Lobster Press™
1620 Sherbrooke Street West, Suites C & D
Montréal, Québec   H3H 1C9
Tel. (514) 904-1100 • Fax (514) 904-1101 • www.lobsterpress.com

Publisher: Alison Fripp
Editor: William Mersereau
Graphic design & production: Tammy Desnoyers
Cover design: Marielle Maheu

We acknowledge the financial support of the Government of Canada through the Book
Publishing Industry Development Program (BPIDP) for our publishing activities.

We acknowledge the support of the Canada
Council for the Arts for our publishing program.

The Canada Council   Le Conseil des Arts
for the Arts   du Canada

National Library of Canada Cataloguing in Publication Data

Wiebe, Trina, 1970-
    Parrots don't make house calls / by Trina Wiebe ; illustrations by Marisol Sarrazin.

(Abby and Tess, pet-sitters, ISSN 1499-9412 ; 7)
ISBN 978-1-894222-45-7

    I. Sarrazin, Marisol, 1965- II. Title. III. Series: Wiebe, Trina, 1970- .
Abby and Tess, pet-sitters ; 7.

PS8595.I358P37 2003   jC813'.6   C2003-902653-1
PZ7

Printed and bound in the United States.

Contents

1 Make Way for Baby

"Why can't I have a slumber party?" complained Abby. She reached into the cardboard box and pulled out her old fuzzy yellow baby blanket printed with green elephants. She hadn't seen it in years. "Everybody else has sleepovers. I've already gone to two at Rachel's house this summer."

Mom folded a tiny pair of pajamas. "We've been over this a hundred times, Abby. There's just not enough room here for a slumber party."

"I hate this rotten apartment," grumbled Abby. "I can't do anything fun here. It's not fair."

"You could invite Rachel over to watch a video," suggested Mom. "You haven't done that in ages."

"Videos are for babies, and I'm nearly eleven!" wailed Abby. "I want a real slumber party. With nine or ten girls. We could stay up till midnight and watch real movies and eat popcorn and play games. Truth or Dare is boring with two people."

Mom took the elephant blanket from Abby and folded it into a neat square. "Where exactly would you like everyone to sleep?" she asked with a patient smile. "There's barely enough room for you and Tess in your bedroom as it is. Are you going to put a couple of girls out in the hallway? Maybe ask one of them to sleep under the kitchen table? How about the bathtub? That sounds comfortable."

Abby snatched a bib from the box and glared at it. "Very funny, Mom. Why can't we sleep in the living room?"

Mom looked around the living room that was filled with a jumble of cardboard boxes and shook her head.

"Sorry, kiddo. I've got to store my art supplies and paint and paper somewhere until I can move it into my new studio at the community college. And we'll have to hurry," she added, putting one hand on the swell of her stomach, "if we want to convert my home studio into a nursery before the baby is born."

Abby bit her lip. She and her younger sister Tess had been thrilled when their parents announced that a baby was on the way. Tess had been so thrilled, in fact, that she'd started acting even weirder than usual. For one thing, she barked like crazy whenever she caught a glimpse of a baby in the park or at the mall, and would run over to sniff it. Abby was used to Tess's quirky canine behavior, and the babies didn't seem to mind, but they got some pretty strange looks from the mothers.

Abby had been excited about the baby news, too. She couldn't wait to have a wonderful new brother or sister to play with and look after and teach things to. It was almost like getting a pet, only better. Lately, though, Abby had begun to see that things were going to change in other ways too — and not in the ways she had hoped.

She had thought a new baby would mean moving into a bigger apartment, or maybe even buying a house of their own with a basement and a backyard and everything. The apartment they lived in now was cramped and the building had a dumb No Pets Allowed rule.

Abby hated that rule. It was the worst rule imaginable when you loved animals as much as she did. The only way she could spend time with animals was to run her own pet-sitting business, with Tess as her helper. It was a lot of fun, and they'd looked after all kinds of cool pets, from ants to lizards to pot-bellied pigs! They had even spent two weeks of their summer vacation on Gran's farm, taking care of an adorable baby goat named Missy. Pet-sitting was almost as good as having your own pets — but not quite. Abby still longed for her own backyard, so she could have her very own puppy. Or kitten. Or maybe a couple of each.

Unfortunately they weren't moving anywhere. Dad said adding another person to their family meant it was going to take even longer to save up enough money for a house. The apartment, which already felt crowded to Abby, was going to feel like one of those teeny tiny circus cars that held a whole bunch of clowns. Mom would have to give up her studio and work on her art at the community college where she taught classes, just so the baby could have a nursery. Abby and Tess would continue to share a cramped bedroom.

And slumber parties would still be impossible.

"It's just not fair," repeated Abby. She frowned and folded her arms over her chest. "Why does the baby get your studio? Why can't I have it?"

Mom stopped folding miniature undershirts and looked at Abby. "I understand how you feel," she said. "Really, I do. But a newborn wakes up at all hours of the night and the nursery needs to be close to my bedroom. Maybe, if the baby is a girl, in a year or two she can move in with Tess and then you can have your own room . . ."

Abby slumped against the box of baby clothes. "In a year or two?"

"Sorry, Abby," said Mom, shaking out the last of the baby blankets. "That's just the way it is. With a new baby on the way, we're all going to have to make sacrifices."

Abby grunted.

Mom raised one eyebrow, then continued as though she hadn't noticed. "Thank you for helping me bring these baby clothes up," she said, stacking the folded piles neatly back into the box. "They've been downstairs in our storage locker for so many years I wasn't sure if they'd still be any good. I know we've got plenty of time to worry about things like baby clothes, but I just get so excited thinking about the future. Things are sure going to change around here."

Yeah, thought Abby. For the worse.

2 A Super Special Job

"Woof, woof!" barked Tess. She jumped onto the bed, pawed the back of Abby's shirt, then nosed her sister's elbow. "Supper time!"

Abby grimaced and jerked her arm away. "Yuck," she said. "Why is your nose all wet?"

Tess grinned. "Dogs with wet noses are healthy."

Abby didn't ask where the moisture came from. She wasn't sure she wanted to know. Instead, she wiped her elbow on her shirt and put aside the book she'd been reading.

"What's that?" asked Tess.

Abby shrugged. "A book from the library. It's called *Career Dogs*. You know, like search and rescue dogs. Or those drug-sniffing dogs at the airport."

"Does it have police dogs, too?" Tess said as she cocked her head and grabbed the book. "Because that's what I want to be when I grow up."

"These are dog careers," repeated Abby.

Tess panted and nodded agreeably. "I know."

Abby sighed. Sometimes she wondered if

Tess actually forgot she was a little girl, and not a canine. "Come on," she said, swinging her legs off the bed. "Let's go before supper gets cold."

But Tess wasn't interested in supper anymore. She flipped through the pages of the book, stopping to stare at a glossy photo of a seeing eye dog in a brown leather harness.

"Are you coming?" asked Abby when she reached the door.

Tess didn't answer.

Abby could hear her parents talking and dishes clanking in the kitchen. Shaking her head, she reached into her pocket for the small rubber ball she always kept there. It came in handy sometimes, especially when she was in a rush and Tess was being goofy. If you can't beat them, Abby thought to herself, you might as well play along, even if it made you look silly.

"Here, Tess. Fetch!" she cried, first showing her sister the rubber ball, then tossing it out the door and down the hall toward the kitchen.

Tess snapped to attention. She flew after the ball like a missile homing in on its target. Abby followed behind and when she arrived in the kitchen she found the whole family at the table, waiting for her.

Dad winked at Abby and held out his hand. "I believe this belongs to you."

Abby took the rubber ball and squeezed into her empty chair. "Thanks," she muttered, shoving the ball into her pocket.

"So how was work, dear?" Mom asked, passing a bowl of steamed turnips to Dad. He'd recently started working as an assistant physical therapist at the hospital. It was his job to help people learn to use their bodies again after being hurt or sick.

"Fine," said Dad. He took the turnips, wrinkled his nose, but spooned some onto his plate and passed the dish to Abby. Mom had been cooking all kinds of weird vegetables lately. They were good for the baby.

Abby held her breath and put a tiny yellow chunk on the edge of her plate. She understood turnips were high in vitamins, but why did they have to smell so icky? Still holding her breath, she quickly shoved the bowl toward Tess.

Tess took one whiff and threw back her head to let out one of her famous ear-splitting howls. Dad glanced at Mom and grabbed the bowl.

"Actually," he said quickly, "something interesting did happen at work today. I was saving it for a surprise. I think there might be a temporary job for you girls at the hospital."

Tess forgot about the turnips. "Really?"

Abby looked up from the table, where she had managed to hide her turnip in her folded napkin. "What kind of job?"

"A pet-sitting job, of course," said Dad. He took a bite of turnip, chewed once, then shoved a forkful of pasta into his mouth. Swallowing hard, he smiled at his wife. "Delicious."

Mom raised one eyebrow. "Vitamin C," she

said. "Good for the . . ."

"Baby," Abby groaned, finishing the sentence for her. She was beginning to get tired of hearing that. "If it's good for the baby, then why do we have to eat it too?"

"About the job," continued Dad, "have you girls ever heard of Animal-Assisted Activity?"

Abby sat up straighter in her chair. Hadn't she just read something about that in her *Career Dogs* book? She wrinkled her nose, thinking hard.

"Is that where people take dogs into hospitals to cheer up the patients?" she asked. The idea of working with a dog gave her a tingly feeling in her stomach.

Dad nodded. "Not only hospitals, but also nursing homes and group homes and psychiatric facilities. You'd be amazed at how good animals are at helping people get better."

"Doggy doctors," said Tess with a giggle. "That's funny."

Dad smiled. "That's right, Tess, but it's not just dogs . . ."

"Don't you need special training to do that?" interrupted Abby.

Dad nodded and his face grew serious. "Yes,

you do. Volunteers must be screened and certified and attend training seminars. We have to make sure our patients, and the animals, are safe at all times."

Abby's shoulders slumped. "I thought so. So what does this have to do with us?"

"Well," said Dad, pushing his plate aside and leaning forward to look into Abby's face. "We've got a special situation at the hospital right now, and I think you and Tess would be perfect for the job."

3 Doctor Doggy

"What kind of special situation?" asked Abby. She felt her hopes rising again.

Dad leaned back in his chair and tapped his fingers on the table. "It's kind of sad, actually. We've got a boy at the hospital who isn't responding to treatment." He noticed Tess's confused face and explained, "He's not getting better and we don't know why."

"What's wrong with him?" asked Tess. "Does he have worms? Because the vet can fix that, you know."

Dad chuckled. "Nope, no worms. He broke his leg in a car accident, but that's not the problem."

"So what is it?" asked Abby. She moved her hand impatiently, uncovering her hidden turnip. With a quick glance at Mom, she shoved it back under the napkin.

"We don't know," said Dad. He shook his head. "My guess is depression. His father severely injured in the accident. He's actually in a coma. The son refuses to speak, get out of bed or do his therapy. We're very worried about him."

"How can we help?" asked Abby.

"Well, we thought he might respond to Animal-Assisted Activity," explained Dad. "The hospital has used animals in the past with stroke victims and terminally ill patients, as well as people with depression. We've arranged for a man named Bob Higgins, who works with a group called Pet Partners, to start visiting the boy."

"Is it working?" asked Abby. She pictured a sad, lonely little boy, huddled in a corner of his hospital bed. A lump formed in her throat.

Dad lifted one hand in the air, then let it drop. "Not really," he admitted. "But we've only just started and I'm positive, given more time, this boy would have responded."

Abby caught her breath. "What do you mean, would have?"

"That's the problem," said Dad. "Bob is going back to England for two weeks, and there's no one to take his place. Which means no more AAA visits. Unless . . ."

Abby clutched the edge of her seat. "I'll do it!" she cried. "Please, Daddy, let me try."

"Me too, me too," squeaked Tess. She banged her fork against her drinking glass and chanted, "Doctor Doggy! Doctor Doggy!"

Dad chuckled. "I knew you girls would be perfect for the job," he said. "There are just a few things you should know . . ."

An awful thought struck Abby. "I know . . . we're not certified."

"I thought of that," said Dad. "We've talked it over and decided that in this unique situation, it would be acceptable as long as there is an adult supervisor with you. And since it was my idea in the first place, I thought I'd take you by every two days after work . . ."

"Thank you Daddy," cried Abby. "Thank you, thank you, thank you!" She jumped up from her chair and threw her arms around him, knocking her napkin — and the turnip — to the floor. The unwanted chunk of vegetable bounced across the linoleum.

"I've arranged to see Bob tomorrow, so you can meet your assistance animal and get instructions," said Dad. "From there we'll go straight to the hospital. How does that sound?"

"Fantastic!" said Abby. She got up and tossed the turnip into the garbage, then returned to the table to finish her supper. Another turnip sat on her plate. Abby looked up at Mom, who smiled.

Abby shrugged, then stabbed the vegetable with her fork and nibbled on it. Not even smelly vegetables could spoil her good mood tonight. This pet-sitting job would be the perfect chance to spend time with a wonderful, lovable dog, not to mention get away from the apartment for awhile.

She couldn't wait for tomorrow!

4 Squawky Surprise

"Here we are," said Dad the next afternoon. He glanced in his rearview mirror, signaled, and pulled the car over to the curb.

"But this is an apartment complex," Abby said, frowning. She stared at the tall, gray concrete building. "How can they have a dog when they don't even have a backyard?"

"Listen, Abby . . ." began Dad.

"It must be a small dog," Abby decided, getting out of the car. "One of the toy breeds, maybe, like a Chihuahua or a Pekinese. You probably wouldn't want a big hairy sheepdog in the hospital, after all."

"I like sheepdogs," objected Tess. She hopped onto the sidewalk beside Abby.

"Actually, big dogs are often used in animal assistance activities," Dad told them. "From what Bob says, there are a number of large animals involved with Pet Partners. Why, they even have a llama."

Tess's mouth fell open. "A llama?"

"He's teasing you," said Abby with a snort.

Dad crossed his heart with one finger. "I swear

it's true. Lucy the llama especially loves riding up and down hospital elevators."

"If you say so," said Abby. Sometimes it was hard to tell when he was pulling her leg. She looked back at the building. "There definitely isn't room for a llama here, or a sheepdog either. Maybe it's a toy poodle, or . . ."

"A parrot," said Dad.

Abby paused, then laughed. "Good one, Dad."

"I tried to tell you last night," said Dad with a small shrug. "Bob's assistance animal is an African gray parrot named Chiku."

Abby stared at Dad. Her excitement over pet-sitting a dog evaporated. "Really?"

Dad nodded. "I met her, and believe me, she's quite a talented bird. She can imitate almost any sound she hears."

Abby thought about this as she followed Dad into the building. She'd seen parrots in the pet store before, and she'd always liked the intelligent way they looked back at her. Maybe this job would be interesting after all, dogs or no dogs.

The elevator pinged when they reached the fourth floor. Dad stopped in front of a door marked "4C" and rapped on it three times.

Nothing happened.

"We're right on time," said Dad, checking his watch.

"Shhh," said Tess. She pointed her ear toward the door. "I hear something!"

Abby rolled her eyes. It didn't take super sensitive ears to detect the squeals and shouts coming from 4C. A burst of shrill laughter was followed by an enormous thud that rattled the door on its hinges.

Abby winced. "Are you sure this is the right place?"

Dad nodded. "Apartment 4C. I wrote it down."

Shrieks filled the hallway. "Awfully loud parrot," said Abby. She felt Tess slip a small hand into hers.

Dad knocked again, and the door suddenly swung inward. In the doorway stood a goblin in a black robe, its greenish-gray skin peppered with warts. Tess yelped in surprise and even Abby took half a step backward.

"Uh, is Bob Higgins here?" asked Dad.

The hideous creature tugged on its nose. A small boy's face appeared behind the Halloween mask. "Nope," he said. "Want Mum?"

Dad nodded and said, "Yes, that would be . . ."

"MUUUUUUUUM!" shrieked the boy.

"I'm right behind you, dear," said Mrs. Higgins, stepping out from behind her son. Her hair was pulled up in a sloppy ponytail and she carried a baby wearing a droopy diaper and one sock.

"I'm so sorry," she apologized to Abby's dad in a crisp British accent. "I was changing the baby's nappy. Please, come in."

Abby and Tess followed Dad into the apartment, sidling past the boy in the costume. Tess headed straight for the baby, sniffing the toes on its bare foot. The baby giggled and kicked Tess in the nose.

Abby looked around the apartment with interest. A baby swing was crammed into one corner behind a half-built castle of empty milk cartons. A large doll-house teetered on the coffee table, and miniature chairs, beds and even a tiny toilet were strewn across the floor. Someone had pulled most of the books out of a bookcase to form a winding road on the floor for toy cars and trucks.

And she thought their apartment was crowded!

"I'm afraid Bob had to leave early," explained

Mrs. Higgins as she jiggled the baby on her hip. It drooled and stared at Tess. "But he mentioned you'd be stopping by."

A small girl raced into the room. "Mum! Georgie called me a pipsqueak!"

"Did not!" shrieked a voice from another room.

"Did too!" screamed the girl.

"He left instructions," continued Mrs. Higgins, ignoring the girl, who was now tugging on her free arm. The baby started to fuss. "I know the paper is around here somewhere."

Abby felt a giggle bubble up inside her as she watched the boy in the mask, presumably George, sneak up and fire a raisin at his sister.

"You big spaghetti-head!" she squealed, chasing him out of the room.

"Maybe we've come at a bad time," said Dad.

George streaked past them, howling like a banshee, his sister two steps behind. They disappeared around a corner.

"Not at all," Mrs. Higgins assured him. "It's always a bit of a zoo around here. As you can see, we've outgrown our apartment."

"I know the feeling," muttered Abby.

Mrs. Higgins turned to her. "Beg your pardon?"

Abby felt her face go red. "Nothing. I mean, where's the parrot? I'm dying to meet her."

"Ah, yes," said Mrs. Higgins with a laugh. She led them to a small room off the living room. "Every zoo needs a parrot, and ours is right through here."

5 Cheeky Chiku

"Don't be shy, girls," said Mrs. Higgins. "Come in and meet Chiku."

Tess stayed close to Dad, but Abby stepped up to the enormous steel cage that hung from the ceiling. It reminded Abby of a playpen, filled with colorful wooden blocks and plastic dinosaurs and balls filled with holes like Swiss cheese. It even had something that looked like a baby mobile, made of rope and chunky plastic beads hanging from the roof of the cage. In the middle of everything, perched on a wooden swing, sat Chiku.

"Hello, Chiku," Abby said softly.

Chiku angled her head to view Abby with one bright eye. Her body was covered with gray feathers, although Abby noticed that there was a ring of white feathers around her eye. She was surprised to see that her tail wasn't gray, too, but a brilliant shade of red. Chiku flapped her wings twice, then settled down to stare again.

"Chiku is an African gray parrot," explained Mrs. Higgins. "They're thought to be the most intelligent species of parrot. In fact, studies show that they are as smart as primates and porpoises . . ."

George darted into the room, slammed the door, and held onto the doorknob with both hands while his sister pounded on the opposite side. Mrs. Higgins sighed and added, "Or small children."

"Can she talk?" Abby asked.

Dad and Mrs. Higgins looked at each other and laughed. "She certainly can," said Dad. "She's got quite a colorful vocabulary. Go ahead, ask her something."

"Um, how are you, Chiku?" Abby said, addressing the parrot. She waited for an answer but Chiku remained silent. Abby tried again. "Are you hungry?"

Chiku squawked.

"Sometimes she's shy at first," said Mrs. Higgins. "I think she misses Bob. Often African grays pick one person in the family as their favorite. They're very loyal birds. But once Chiku gets to know you, she'll talk your ear off."

"Can I touch her?" asked Abby.

"Sure," said Mrs. Higgins. She thrust the baby

into Dad's arms and turned to fiddle with the latch on Chiku's cage. Dad and the baby stared at each other for a shocked moment, then the baby opened its mouth to wail. Abby braced herself, but the baby grabbed a fistful of Dad's shirt. Tess snickered as the baby stuffed it into its mouth and sucked on it.

Abby turned away to hide her smirk and saw that Chiku was now out of her cage, perched on Mrs. Higgins's wrist. She gasped. Chiku was so beautiful! Abby could almost imagine her flying wild through the African Congo.

"During the hospital visits, Chiku should probably remain in her traveling cage," said Mrs. Higgins. "But you can hold her now, if you like."

Abby suddenly felt nervous. What if Chiku didn't like her? "Does she bite?" she asked, remembering Mrs. Nibbles, the class hamster she had looked after during spring break.

"Well, sometimes," said Mrs. Higgins. She smiled at Abby. "Just don't make any sudden moves. You don't want to startle her. Take it nice and easy and I'm sure you'll be great chums."

Mrs. Higgins instructed Abby to hold out her arm, slightly higher than her own. Chiku lifted one clawed foot and gingerly stepped up. Abby's arm grew heavy under the extra weight, and she struggled to hold it steady.

"Try rubbing her head," suggested Mrs. Higgins. "She likes that."

Abby slowly brought her other hand up and lightly touched the back of the parrot's neck. Chiku didn't seem to mind, so she petted the white feathers on her face.

"Nice girl," Abby crooned. "Aren't you a pretty thing."

Chiku twisted her neck and rubbed her cheek against Abby's hand. "'Ello, luv!" she said in a scratchy voice.

Abby gasped again. She looked at Dad and Tess in amazement. "Did you hear that?"

Dad shifted his grip on the squirming baby and grinned. "I think you've got a friend, Abby."

"My turn!" cried Tess. She jumped up and down. "Me next! Woof, woof!"

Chiku suddenly propelled herself into the air in a flurry of beating wings. Screeching terribly, she circled the room, finally landing on top of her cage. She eyed Tess and flapped her wings threateningly.

Tess yelped and hid behind Dad.

"Cheeky monkey!" Chiku hissed at Tess. "Cheeky monkey!"

6 Pet Partners

"Well, I think she's cheeky," said Tess, crossing her arms and scowling fiercely. She slouched in the back seat of the car behind Dad, leaning as far away from Chiku as possible. She hadn't looked at Chiku once while Mrs. Higgins put her in the traveling cage, an ordinary-looking, round-topped wire cage, and brought her down to the car.

"She didn't mean it," objected Abby. "You just scared her, that's all." Chiku's traveling cage sat in the back seat between the sisters, held securely in place with the seatbelt. A towel was draped over the cage to help keep Chiku warm and calm. Mrs. Higgins had warned Abby that birds must be kept out of the wind as they chill very easily, even in summer.

Tess pouted and stared out the window. "Well I think she's mean."

Dad drove to the hospital, found a parking spot and turned off the engine.

"So, are you girls ready for your first Pet Partner visit?" he asked.

Abby unbuckled Chiku's cage. "You bet."

Tess grunted.

They entered the wide front doors of the hospital and followed Dad through a maze of beige corridors, up an elevator and into another hallway. The walls of this hallway were different from the rest of the hospital. Purple monkeys and blue elephants romped in a painted jungle mural.

"Look," said Abby, pointing. "There's a parrot."

Tess sniffed and stared straight ahead. "Parrots are dopey," she muttered.

After signing in at the nursing station, Dad stopped in front of a closed door. "This is Elliot's room," he said. He put out an arm to stop Tess from pushing the door open. "Don't be upset if he doesn't talk to you or even look at you. Just be yourselves."

Abby patted Chiku's cage. "Don't worry, Dad, nobody can resist Chiku."

Tess sniffed again, but didn't say anything.

"Okay, then," said Dad. "Let's give this a try."

Dad entered the room first, then Tess, and Abby carried Chiku in last. It was a private room with a single bed. In the bed was a thin boy about Abby's age. He lay on top of the neatly arranged covers, his arms flat on the blankets on either side of his body. He wore blue pajamas and one leg was covered up to the knee in a thick, white cast.

"Girls, this is Elliot," introduced Dad. "Elliot, these are my daughters, Abby and Tess. They've brought Chiku to visit you while Mr. Higgins is away."

Elliot stared at the ceiling.

Abby bit her lip, then stepped forward. "Hi," she said.

Elliot didn't respond. It was like Abby was invisible. She glanced at Dad, who gave her an encouraging nod. She took a deep breath and tried again.

"Do you want me to take the towel off of Chiku's cage?" she asked. "We can't let her out, but we can look at her through the bars."

Abby waited a moment, then set the traveling cage on a wheeled hospital table that made a bridge over the end of Elliot's bed. Slowly, she pulled off the towel. Chiku squawked and hopped closer to the bars to watch them.

"She can talk," Abby said. "But I guess you already know that, since she's visited you before."

Elliot blinked, but didn't answer.

Tess wasn't interested in Chiku. She spied a pair of wooden crutches leaning against the wall. "Can I try those?" she asked.

Dad shook his head. "They belong to Elliot."

Tess sighed, then spotted a plastic cord sprouting from the wall. There was a round, knobby button on the end that was clipped to the bed beside Elliot's pillow. "What's that?" she asked.

"The call button," Dad said, catching Tess's elbow. "Don't touch. It's for emergencies only."

Tess groaned and sank back in the chair. The room grew quiet. Abby wondered if Elliot even knew they were there.

Tess groaned again, louder than before. "This is boring."

"What about a game of checkers?" asked Dad. "I think there's a set in the lounge. It's just down the hall. I'll run and get it."

Dad left and the silence grew uncomfortable. Abby sneaked a peek at Elliot. He hadn't moved since they came in.

Abby tried to think of something else to say, but her mind was blank. Tess could be annoying sometimes, but at least she always had something to say. Even barking was better than this!

Abby tried to signal Tess with her eyes. "Say something," she mouthed.

Tess glanced at Chiku, sniffed, then turned her back and pulled open the night table drawers.

Abby walked over and slammed them shut. "Quit snooping," she hissed. "I know you don't like Chiku, but we're on the job, remember? Now get over here and help me out."

Tess reluctantly let Abby drag her to the bed. When she got close to Chiku, however, the parrot hopped from one foot to the other.

"Cheeky monkey, cheeky monkey!" she squawked.

"I'm not a monkey, you dumb bird!" shouted Tess. "And I'm not cheeky!"

Chiku bobbed her head back and forth. "Pipsqueak!"

Tess growled.

Chiku growled back.

Abby glanced nervously at the door. How long did it take to get a checkerboard? "Knock it off, you guys," she said. "We're in a hospital, remember?"

"Woof, woof!" barked Tess, glaring at the parrot.

"Woof-woof!" mimicked Chiku.

"We're going to get kicked out," moaned Abby. She couldn't believe this was happening on the first day of the new job. Tess was supposed to be her pet-sitting partner, but right now Abby felt like she was taking care of two animals, not just one. "Would you two put a sock in it, already?"

"Copycat!" cried Tess.

"Copycat!" retorted Chiku.

Abby thought she heard a noise from the bed, but just then the door opened and Dad walked in.

"How's everything going in here?" he asked.

7 A Tough Nut to Crack

"It's going great," muttered Abby. She glanced at Elliot. He stared blankly at the ceiling. "Just great."

Dad looked from Tess's glowering face to Chiku's ruffled feathers. He smiled brightly and held up a box. "I couldn't find checkers, but I did find a chess board. Who's up for a game?"

"Me, me, me!" said Tess. "I'm super good at chess."

"Good," said Dad. He opened the box and arranged the pieces on another tall, wheeled table. He swiveled the tabletop around so that it was between him and Abby.

Tess dragged her chair closer. "Okay. It's me, Dad and Elliot against Abby." She shot Chiku a dirty look. "You don't count."

Abby opened her mouth to say chess wasn't a team sport, but decided against it. This whole visit was pretty bizarre, why should the chess game be any different?

"We go first!" decided Tess. She looked all around the board, then peeked under the table.

"Where's the dice?"

Abby thought she heard another snort from Elliot's direction. But when she glanced at him, he didn't appear to be paying attention.

"Your move," announced Tess. Abby turned back to the game. The black king and three pawns sat in the center of the board. Abby's white queen was missing.

"Give me a break," she said. "You can't move four men in one turn. That's impossible."

Dad shrugged helplessly. "I think we're playing by Tess Rules."

Abby frowned. She knew from experience that it was impossible to win any game played with "Tess Rules." No matter what you did, Tess always won. It was a big waste of time.

Just then a clanking noise caught Abby's attention. Chiku was at her cage door, banging on the metal bars with her beak.

"I think she wants out," Abby said, looking at Dad.

Dad shook his head. "No, we'd better not. Bob thought we should keep her in the cage during these visits, at least at first. Chiku doesn't really know us yet, and . . ."

"Oh, please, Dad?" begged Abby. "The windows and door are shut. She can't escape. Besides, she likes me."

Tess pouted.

"I don't know," said Dad.

Chiku pecked at the door again. "Out!" she demanded.

Dad stared at the bird in surprise.

"I say, chaps," said Chiku in her scratchy voice, "anyone for footie?"

"What's 'footie'?" asked Abby.

"She must mean soccer," said Dad. "They call it football in England."

"Out!" insisted Chiku. "Let's have a kick around!"

Dad hesitated, glanced at Abby's pleading face, then finally relented. "Just for a little while, then."

Abby grinned and unlatched the door. Chiku twisted her neck to gaze at her with one eye, then daintily stepped out of the cage. She hopped from the table onto Abby's knee and surveyed the chess game.

"Your turn," muttered Tess.

Abby didn't care about the game anymore.

She was far more interested in the parrot on her knee. But she reached out and moved one of her pawns forward.

Tess clapped her hands gleefully. "A-ha! You fell into my trap," she crowed. "Gimme both of your horses and that castle guy too."

"Go ahead and take them," said Abby, studying Chiku. Up close, she was fairly big, for a bird. Her beak was black and curved downward, with a rough edge that looked like it could crack open the toughest nuts.

"It's your turn again," said Tess.

Abby reached to move a chess piece at random, but Chiku beat her to it. She flap-hopped onto the table and pushed Abby's rook forward with one claw. "Score!" she squawked.

Tess's cheeks flushed pink. "That's cheating," she said. "You can't move there."

"Now, Tess," began Dad, putting one hand on Tess's shoulder. "She's just a bird . . ."

"Just a bird, just a bird!" screeched Chiku. "Let's play footie!" She hopped forward and knocked over Tess's king. It rolled off the table and clattered to the floor.

"No fair," cried Tess.

"Spaghetti-head!" croaked Chiku.

This time Abby was certain she heard a noise. She turned her head quickly and Elliot's face resumed its usual blank expression, but not before she'd caught the tiniest glimpse of a smile.

8 The Key

"I think that's enough chess for one day," said Dad. He swept the game pieces back into the box. "We'll play again on our next visit."

Carefully, Abby coaxed Chiku back into her cage, which she latched and covered with the towel. She watched Elliot out of the corner of her eye. Dad and Tess left the room, but Abby lingered behind. "See you in two days," she said to Elliot.

He blinked, then rolled on his side to stare out the window.

Instead of feeling snubbed, however, Abby felt a wave of sympathy. How lonely Elliot must be. Scared, too. Abby sighed and carried Chiku's cage into the hall where Dad and Tess were waiting.

"Ready to go?" asked Dad. He glanced at his watch. "We've got just enough time to take Chiku back and make it home for supper."

Abby nodded, her mind still on Elliot. He'd been listening, all right. She was certain she'd heard him almost laugh. It wasn't much, but it was a start.

When they arrived at Chiku's building, Tess refused to leave the car.

"I won't go up there," she said, crossing her arms over her chest. "Not until she apologizes."

"That's silly, Tess," said Dad. "She's a bird, for goodness sake."

"She called me spaghetti-head," pouted Tess.

Dad looked helplessly at Abby.

"I'll take her up," Abby offered. When Tess got that stubborn look in her eyes, it would be easier to move a mountain than to get her to change her mind.

Dad hesitated. "Do you remember which apartment it is?"

Abby was already unbuckling Chiku's cage. "Yup. I'll be back in a flash," she promised.

Chiku squawked a bit when they stepped into the elevator, but Abby talked to her in a gentle voice until she calmed down. She found apartment 4C and knocked on the door.

"Who is it?" yelled someone through the closed door.

"It's me, Abby," she called back, recognizing George's voice. "I'm here to drop off Chiku."

"Hang on," George shouted. Muffled footsteps thudded inside the apartment. A moment later, he opened the door. "Mum's in the shower," he said, "but she said you can come in."

Abby followed him into the kitchen. His little sister was at the table, drawing. She looked up when Abby entered, then went back to her picture, the tip of her tongue showing between her lips as she scribbled madly with a green crayon.

George pointed to a small table by a window. "Just put her over there," he instructed.

Abby set Chiku on the table. Beneath it, she noticed a bag of brownish pellets. She knelt down to look more closely at the parrot supplies. Beside the pellets sat a large squirt bottle marked "cage cleaner" and a smaller bottle filled with something called "organic fruit and vegetable soap."

Suddenly she realized she didn't know anything at all about African gray parrots. Usually when she had a pet-sitting job, she tried to learn everything she could about the animal. Sure, this was a special job, and she wasn't taking care of Chiku full time. Still, she felt like she should know more about her. She made a mental note to ask Dad to stop at the library on their way home.

"What's this for?" she asked George, pointing to the soap.

George shrugged. "I dunno."

His sister giggled. "George doesn't know anything."

"I know more than you do, crayon-face!" George shot back.

This must be the way they always talk to each other Abby thought in amazement. Tess was annoying sometimes with her strange doggy mannerisms, but at least she wasn't always throwing around insults.

Abby stood up. "I have to go. My dad's waiting downstairs. Tell your mom we'll be back the day after tomorrow, okay?"

"Sure," shrugged George. He leaned against the kitchen table and deliberately jiggled it.

"Hey!" cried his sister. "You made me color outside the lines!"

Abby let herself out. Before the apartment door closed behind her, she heard names like "crayon-face" and "spaghetti-head" flying around the kitchen. It was easy to see where Chiku picked up her vocabulary.

In the elevator, Abby's thoughts returned to Elliot. He was like a bank vault, locked up tight. There had to be a way to unlock him.

She remembered how Elliot had almost laughed today. Chiku just might be the key.

9 Zzzzz . . . Another Failure

"Wake up, sleepyhead," whispered Mom two days later.

Abby groaned. Usually she was the first person up in the mornings, but she'd stayed up until almost midnight reading library books about African gray parrots under the covers with a flashlight. Now she felt awful.

"You gave me the most wonderful idea yesterday," Mom said. She sat on the edge of Abby's bed. The extra weight of her belly made the mattress sink lower than usual. "And I need your help to make it work."

Abby opened one eye. "What idea?"

"When you described the hospital mural," said Mom, "I realized that's exactly what our nursery needs."

Abby opened the other eye. "Purple monkeys?"

"No, silly," grinned Mom. "I was thinking of an enchanted forest, with wildflowers and toadstools and pixies. Wouldn't that be lovely?"

Abby sat up and nodded. It did sound nice.

She wouldn't mind having a room like that herself. But this was for the baby, of course.

As usual.

"But I'm not an artist," she grumbled. "How can I help?"

An hour later, she was sorry she'd asked. Abby and Tess spent the whole afternoon preparing the walls for the mural. They scrubbed them. They scraped them. They rinsed them and dried them and helped prime them with a base coat of white paint. By the time Dad got home from work, Abby felt about as energetic as a limp dishrag.

"What's going on in here?" asked Dad, stepping into the soon-to-be nursery. He hugged Mom. "I thought you were going to rest today."

Mom gave him one end of a tube of paper. "I've got all this energy suddenly," she said. She unrolled the paper, revealing a rough pencil sketch of the mural. "What do you think?"

Dad studied the drawing. "It's gorgeous. But it looks like a lot of work."

"The girls are helping," said Mom.

"It's for the baby," muttered Abby. She turned away and pretended to have trouble with a paint can lid so that her parents couldn't see her face. She banged the lid shut, using more force than necessary.

"Well, I think you've done enough for one day," said Dad. He rolled up the sketch and pulled the pencil from behind Mom's ear. "Time for a cup of tea. Doctor's orders."

"Finally," groaned Tess. She crawled across the floor, too tired to even bark. Her face and clothes were streaked with paint.

"You girls get cleaned up," said Dad. "We'll pick up Chiku in half an hour."

Tess scowled and headed for the bathroom. Abby washed up next, then went to their bedroom. Maybe Elliot would like to learn more about parrots, too. She felt her energy level rising as she packed her library books into a bag. She was sure she'd break through his silence this time!

At the hospital, Abby pushed open Elliot's door and stepped inside. Nothing seemed to have changed since they left him. Elliot lay in the bed, arms neatly by his sides, as though the nurses had smoothed and arranged him and the blankets at the same time. The crutches leaned in the same spot against the wall, untouched.

Dad and Tess sat in the chair and Abby set Chiku's cage on the hospital table. She removed the towel so Chiku could see.

"Hi Elliot," she said. "I brought you something."

Elliot didn't look at her. Abby sat beside Chiku and reached into her book bag. She pulled out the first one her fingers touched. It was a slim book called *How to Care for Your Parrot.*

"This is a good one," she said. "It has lots of pictures. Should I read it out loud?"

"That's a great idea," said Dad, when Elliot didn't answer. Tess got comfortable in Dad's lap and yawned.

Abby glanced at Elliot again. The frown on his face looked like it was carved in cement. Had she imagined that smile the other day?

She took a deep breath and started reading. The book explained all about how parrots need to eat a variety of healthy foods, and how fruits and vegetables must be peeled or washed thoroughly in order to get rid of chemicals that might make them sick. Abby smiled, thinking that the mystery of the organic soap was solved.

When she finished the book, she put it down and chose another one with a photo of an African gray on the cover. This one was more like a textbook, with pages and pages of words. Abby skimmed through it.

"Listen to this," she said, finding an interesting bit. "It says here that the African gray parrot is native to the jungles of central Africa, where it was hunted for food and for its beautiful tail feathers that were thought to be magical."

She turned the page, engrossed in her research. "It also says that they were taken aboard ships to be sold as pets in Europe, as early as the mid 1800s. They were packed into long tubes and many didn't survive the journey because people didn't believe they needed water. Talk about lousy pet-sitters!"

Abby flipped ahead. "Oh, cool," she said, running her fingers down the page. "There's an African gray parrot at a university that can count up to six, knows his colors and can name nearly a hundred objects! Mrs. Higgins wasn't kidding when she said Chiku was smart."

Abby chuckled and looked up to see what the others thought. Tess was curled up in Dad's arms, snoring softly. Dad's head was tipped forward. Elliot's eyes were closed. Even Chiku seemed to be napping.

Abby sighed and shut the book. Visit number two looked like a failure, too.

10 Elevators and Parrot Muffins

On Friday afternoon, Dad and Tess waited in the car while Abby rode the elevator up to apartment 4C to get Chiku. This time, Mrs. Higgins answered the door.

"Good to see you Abby," she said with a smile. "Come in. Chiku is all set to go."

Abby followed Mrs. Higgins into the kitchen, where Chiku was waiting in her traveling cage.

"'Ello luv!" she squawked.

Abby giggled. "Hi Chiku," she answered. "Ready to go on a trip?"

"Go on a trip!" repeated Chiku.

At the hospital, Abby carried Chiku's cage while Dad once again led them through the maze of hallways. Soon Abby recognized the jungle mural and they headed toward Elliot's room. When Dad reached the door, Abby grabbed his arm.

"Where's Tess?" she asked.

"What do you mean?" he asked, turning around. Tess was nowhere in sight. Dad frowned. "Where did she go?"

"She was right behind me when we got off the

elevator," said Abby. She shifted her grip on Chiku's cage. "Wasn't she?"

Dad ran his fingers through his hair. He pursed his lips tightly as he strode back down the hallway. Abby hurried to keep up, while trying not to let the cage bump against her legs with every step.

"Why would she stay in the elevator?" he asked. "I told her the fifth floor is the maternity ward, there's nothing up there except . . ."

Abby stopped in her tracks. "The maternity ward?"

Dad glanced at her over his shoulder and stopped too. "That's right."

"She probably wanted to sniff the babies," said Abby. "She likes to do that, you know."

"Sniff the babies?" he repeated, a puzzled frown replacing the worried look on his face.

Abby shrugged. "She's been kind of baby-crazy lately." Just like the rest of the family, she thought to herself. Last night's Brussels sprouts, while high in fiber and potassium, smelled like sweaty gym socks. After that, Mom had pulled out their old baby albums and made them look at boring newborn photos and locks of hair for what seemed like hours.

"Good grief," cried Dad. "I'd better find her, quick!"

"Can I wait in Elliot's room?" asked Abby. She shifted Chiku's traveling cage from one hand to the other. "This bird isn't light, you know."

Dad glanced at the cage, then looked at the elevator down the hall. He hesitated, but finally nodded. "Go straight to Elliot's room and stay put. I don't need two lost daughters wandering around the hospital, okay?"

"Okay," promised Abby. She watched him disappear into the elevator and smiled. Dad was the coolest grown-up she knew, but he was still an adult. If she was going to break through the wall Elliot had built around himself, she had a better chance of doing it alone.

With Chiku's help, of course.

Abby pushed open the door and walked up to Elliot's bed. She put Chiku's cage in its regular spot on the hospital table. "We're back," she announced.

Elliot didn't move. Abby was tempted to hold a mirror under his nose to see if it fogged up.

"I brought Chiku again," she said. "And Mrs. Higgins gave me some parrot snacks. She says it's good to reward Chiku when she learns a new word or does what she's told. You know, positive reinforcement."

Still no reaction from Elliot. Chiku, however, refused to keep quiet any longer.

"Out!" she squawked. "Out, Out!"

"Sorry Chiku, I can't," said Abby. She removed the towel. "Is that better?"

Chiku hopped over to the cage door and tapped it with her beak. "Cor, blimey!" she squawked. "Anyone for footie?"

Abby poked her finger between the metal bars and stroked the parrot's neck. "Sorry," she told her. "We're not playing games today. You have to stay in there."

"Out!" insisted Chiku.

"How about a nice, fresh muffin instead?" offered Abby. She dug into the snack bag and pulled out one of Mrs. Higgins' homemade parrot muffins, baked with sweet potatoes, kidney beans and whole eggs — shells included!

Chiku ignored the muffin and rubbed her face against Abby's fingers. "Please, luv."

"But I can't," said Abby. "Dad and Tess will be here any moment . . ."

"Oh, just let her out already," said Elliot.

11 He Speaks!

Abby whirled around. She was so busy with Chiku that she'd almost forgotten Elliot was in the room.

"What did you say?" she asked.

"Let her out," repeated Elliot. "Open the cage."

Abby lifted her arms helplessly. "But Dad said . . ."

Elliot raised himself up on his elbows and looked straight into Abby's face. "She doesn't like being stuck in there," he said slowly. His eyes were as dark as Chiku's, filled with a pain that Abby didn't think had anything do with his broken leg.

"How would you like to be locked up like that?" he asked. "Alone. Stuck. With everybody staring at you all the time?"

Abby guessed he wasn't talking about the parrot anymore. She felt like she was taking a test. If she did the right thing now, she'd pass. If she did the wrong thing, Elliot would go back into his shell and refuse to talk.

Abby glanced at the door and windows. They

were shut tight. Slowly, she reached out and unlatched the cage. Chiku hopped through the opening and perched on Elliot's cast. She hopped up the length of the cast, stopping at Elliot's knee. The boy and the bird studied each other.

"She doesn't like your little sister much, does she?" asked Elliot after awhile.

Abby grinned. "They didn't exactly hit it off the first time they met. I don't think Chiku is fond of dogs. You probably noticed that Tess is a little, um, unusual."

"She barks," said Elliot.

Abby nodded and sat down on the end of the bed. "And growls and whimpers and scratches her pretend fleas. You should see her when someone throws a stick in the park. It's embarrassing."

Elliot almost smiled.

Abby kept talking, afraid to stop now that she had his attention. "One time she visited a friend's house and found a box of dog biscuits. You know, the kind shaped like little bones? We don't know how many she'd eaten by the time they found her. Tess said she was just cleaning the tartar off her teeth. Mom and Dad had a hard time convincing her to use her toothbrush after that."

Elliot chuckled. "Is that really true?"

Abby copied Dad's gesture, crossing her heart with one finger. "Absolutely," she said. "I'm the only kid in our school who has a little sister that barks at the mailman. Lucky me."

The smile left Elliot's face. "You are lucky."

Abby didn't know what to say. She wondered if Elliot had brothers or sisters, and where his mom was, but she wasn't brave enough to ask. They watched Chiku fly over to the window ledge and inspect the traffic in the street below until there was a knock at the door. Dad stuck his head into the room.

"You were right, Abby, I found Tess at the nurses' station on the fifth floor and they were just about to call security . . ." He broke off when he spotted Chiku's empty cage. "Where's the parrot?"

Abby pointed to Elliot's crutches, where Chiku was now perched. "Don't worry, I made sure the windows were locked," she said quickly. Please don't get mad, she begged him with her eyes.

Dad frowned and opened his mouth, then he noticed Elliot was sitting up in bed. "Our time is up," he said simply. "Better put Chiku back in her cage. Tess and I will wait in the hall."

"Okay, Dad," said Abby. She thought he winked at her before closing the door with a soft click.

"Come on, Chiku," said Abby, standing up. "Let's go for a trip."

"Put a sock in it!" squawked Chiku.

Elliot giggled.

Abby stared at Chiku, remembering their first visit when she told Tess and Chiku to put a sock in it. I'm going to have to be more careful what I say around that bird, she thought.

"Come on, Chiku," she coaxed. "It's time to go home now. Pretty please?"

Chiku flapped her wings, but stayed on the crutches.

"I have an idea," said Elliot. "Bring me the cage."

Abby wheeled the table with the empty cage up to the head of the bed, closer to Elliot. She watched Elliot stretch his arm toward the window. Then he pursed his lips and whistled.

It wasn't a toot-toot train whistle sound, like Abby was expecting, but an amazing bird imitation. Elliot twittered and chirped and warbled so perfectly that it sounded like the room was filled with birds.

Chiku twisted her head to look at Elliot, then flew to his outstretched arm. Elliot gently stroked the feathers on the parrot's head and back. Then he brought the parrot close to the traveling cage door, and Chiku hopped inside.

Abby latched the cage shut. "Thanks," she said. "Where did you learn to whistle like that?"

Elliot slumped back against his pillow. "My Dad taught me."

Abby put the towel on the cage and headed for the door. She didn't ask any more questions. The last thing she wanted was for this visit to end on a sour note.

"Are you coming back next week?" asked Elliot.

Abby paused with her hand on the door handle. "Do you want us to?"

Elliot was quiet, then he nodded.

Abby smiled. "Then we'll be here," she promised.

12 Two Steps Forward, One Back

"It looks like you've made progress with Elliot," said Dad as he slowed the car for a red light. They'd already dropped Chiku off and were now on their way home.

"Yeah. He talked to me," said Abby.

"Really?" asked Dad, giving her a surprised glance. "What did he say?"

"Nothing much," said Abby. "Mostly he listened to me complain about — I mean talk about stuff. But at least he didn't ignore me like usual. That's a good sign, right?"

"That's not good," Dad corrected her. "that's outstanding. You've gotten more results after three visits than the hospital staff has in three weeks."

"It wasn't just me," said Abby. "Chiku helped."

Tess snorted. "How?"

Abby thought about it before answering. "When Elliot watched Chiku, his face just seemed to relax. Scientists have done studies on this, you know. They learned that petting an animal actually lowers a person's blood pressure."

"That's true," agreed Dad. "And for patients with depression, spending time with animals gives them something to focus on other than their problems."

"Even rude animals?" asked Tess.

Dad grinned. "Apparently so."

"Chiku's awfully smart," said Abby. "Sometimes I wonder if she bugs Tess because she knows it will make Elliot laugh. It's like she understands that Elliot needs our help."

"Calling me spaghetti-head isn't smart," said Tess, her lower lip quivering. "It's mean."

"You shouldn't take it so seriously," said Abby. She smiled, remembering how saucy Chiku had been with her today. "She's just repeating what she hears."

"She hurt my feelings," sniffed Tess.

Abby sighed. Then she perked up as an idea

occurred to her. Perhaps what Chiku needed was a little special coaching. "Don't worry," she told Tess. "I have a feeling she'll apologize soon."

On the following Monday afternoon, Tess stayed home to help Mom stencil dragonflies and bumblebees on the nursery walls. Abby didn't object. She was looking forward to spending time with Elliot and Chiku. She just had to figure out a way to get Dad to let her do it alone again.

She brought up the subject in the car. "I hope I can get Elliot to talk to me again today," she said as they neared the hospital.

"I'm sure you will," said Dad. "Just do whatever you did last time."

Abby adjusted the towel on Chiku's cage, which the parrot was picking at through the bars. "Well, that's kind of the thing," she said. "I think Elliot talked to me because we were alone. You know, no adults."

Dad glanced at her in the rearview mirror. "I see."

"It's not that I don't want you there," Abby assured him. "I just think Elliot will be more comfortable if it's just Chiku and me, you know?"

"I guess that makes sense," agreed Dad. "But

these visits are supposed to be supervised, remember?"

Abby nodded. "I know, and I'm not certified."

"However," added Dad with a small shrug of his shoulders. "There's nothing wrong with me popping out to get a snack, is there? And I can't help it if the lineup is especially long, or if I stop to chat with a colleague . . ."

"You're the best, Dad," grinned Abby.

When they arrived at Elliot's room, his face was gloomy, and he stared out the window without greeting them. Abby set Chiku's cage on the table by the bed. Were they back at square one again?

Dad caught her eye. "I'm hungry. Who wants a snack?"

"Tea-time!" squawked Chiku behind the towel. "Bubble and squeak, bubble and squeak!"

"I don't think they have mashed potatoes and cabbage in the vending machine," said Dad with a grin. "How about a chocolate bar instead?"

"I'll have one," said Abby. "Thanks, Dad."

"Out!" demanded Chiku as soon as the door closed behind Dad. "Please, luv."

Abby made sure the hospital room was secure then opened the door, hoping Chiku would work her magic on Elliot. He hadn't looked at them once since they arrived. Chiku hopped out of the cage but didn't approach Elliot.

"Dad's always hungry," said Abby, to fill the silence. "Mom says his stomach is a bottomless pit. Even when we have gross stuff like lima beans." Abby shuddered, remembering last night's supper. "High in fiber but low in taste."

Elliot didn't answer.

Abby bit her lip. Just when she thought she'd made progress with Elliot, he seemed to withdraw. It was like taking two steps forward and one backwards again.

"Tess didn't come," she said. "She's still mad at Chiku. Plus, she's helping Mom with the nursery. Again."

Still no reaction from Elliot.

Abby reached into her pocket and pulled out a bag of sprouted alfalfa seeds. She offered a few to Chiku and watched her snap them up.

"You wouldn't believe this nursery," she told Elliot, saying the first thing that popped into her mind. "Mom painted clouds on the ceiling and the crib looks like it has blackberry vines growing all over it." A note of envy crept into her voice. "My room is plain yellow."

Elliot turned his head to look at her, but Abby didn't notice. She fed more sprouts to Chiku and continued talking.

"I'm ten years old and I have to share a bedroom with Tess," she complained. "This baby isn't even born yet and already it has its own room. It's not fair. Mom spends all her time reading about babies and nutrition and stuff. Dad goes with her to pre-natal classes once a week and Tess keeps coming up with baby names like Spot and Rover and Fido. My whole family is baby crazy and it's driving me nuts!"

Elliot sat up. "Quit complaining," he snapped. "At least you have a family."

13 Apology Lessons

Abby stared at Elliot. Then she leaned forward and put her hand on Elliot's cast. "Your Dad will get better," she told him.

"You don't know that," said Elliot. His voice sounded choked and tight. "Mom died last year and Dad . . . he's all I've got left. Maybe he'll never wake up. Maybe I'll be stuck in this bed forever."

Abby squeezed his hand. She didn't know what to say. She wished now she hadn't told Dad to stay away. "What about your crutches? Can't you walk with them?"

Elliot jerked his hand away. "It's too hard," he said. "Besides, what's the use?"

Chiku hopped to the head of the bed and perched on Elliot's shoulder. "Chin up mate!" she squawked. "Toad in the hole, toad in the hole!"

Elliot looked at Abby and smiled weakly. "What does that mean?"

Abby shrugged. "Who knows? She doesn't always make sense, does she?"

"Nothing makes sense anymore," said Elliot. He sighed and touched Chiku's wing. "But she's right. Feeling bad all the time doesn't help. You know, she's pretty smart for a bird."

"She sure is," agreed Abby. She decided it was time to put her idea into motion. "Want to help me teach her to say she's sorry? I don't think Tess will come back here until she apologizes for calling her a spaghetti-head."

"Well, okay," shrugged Elliot. "How hard could that be?"

By the time Dad returned, Abby and Elliot were red-faced and out of breath from laughing.

"What's going on?" Dad asked.

"We're trying to teach Chiku to apologize," explained Abby. She glanced at Elliot and burst into giggles. "This bird is almost as stubborn as Tess."

"Watch," said Elliot. He held a small piece of broccoli in front of Chiku. "Say 'I'm sorry,'" he instructed.

"God save the Queen!" squawked Chiku, her eye on the broccoli.

"Say, 'I'm sorry,'" repeated Elliot. "Come on, Chiku, say 'I'm sorry.'"

Chiku hopped on one foot and made the sound of a ringing telephone. "Bob's your uncle!" she cried. Then she quacked like a duck.

Abby and Elliot dissolved into giggles.

Dad chuckled too. "Looks like you two have your work cut out for you," he said.

Tess refused to come to the next two visits. Abby and Elliot used that time to continue with their apology lessons. But no matter how many banana chunks or papaya bits they offered, Chiku refused to say those two magic words — I'm sorry.

Abby was still giggling over Chiku's impression of a cuckoo clock when she and Dad drove home after the sixth visit.

"Still no luck with the apology?" asked Dad, slowing for a red light.

Abby patted the traveling cage on the seat beside her and shook her head. "Nope. But Elliot and I are pretty good friends now."

"We're very pleased with Elliot's progress," Dad said. "I'm told he has started opening up in his counseling sessions. Talking about your problems always helps."

"So he's better?" asked Abby.

"Let's just say he's headed in the right direction," said Dad. "You and Chiku are doing a marvelous job."

Abby knew that tone of voice. There was something Dad wasn't telling her. "But?" she prompted.

Dad pulled into a parking spot in front of Chiku's building. He shifted sideways in his seat and looked at Abby.

"The longer Elliot refuses to use his legs, the weaker his muscles become," he said. "Elliot needs to use his crutches — before it's too late."

14 Hospital Hullabaloo

"Come to the hospital with us today, Tess," urged Abby the following Monday afternoon.

Tess squirted more liquid dish soap into the kitchen sink. "Sorry," she said. "I'm too busy cleaning baby toys."

"The baby isn't due for a long time yet," said Abby. "You can wash them later."

Tess picked up a sponge and scrubbed a pink rubber teething toy shaped like teddy bear. It squeaked when she squeezed its middle.

"I want to wash them now," she insisted.

"Come on, it's the last Pet Partner visit. I'll play fetch with you afterwards," Abby promised.

Tess stopped scrubbing. "In the park?"

Abby groaned silently, but nodded. "Sure. In the park."

"Woof! Woof!" barked Tess, splattering soapsuds everywhere. "Let's go!"

Dad drove them to Chiku's building where Abby picked up the parrot. She wasn't entirely sure Chiku would apologize to Tess, but Elliot had insisted that they give it a try. It was now or never.

Bob returned from England tomorrow, and this was Abby and Tess's last pet-sitting day.

At the hospital, Elliot was in bed, as usual, but he smiled when he saw them. Dad spoke with Elliot for a few moments, then excused himself to get a cup of coffee.

Elliot grinned at Tess. "You came this time."

"Abby promised to play with me later," said Tess. She sat in the chair beside the hospital bed and fiddled with the cord of Elliot's call button. "We're going to play fetch. In the park."

"Where everyone can see us," muttered Abby.

Elliot grinned. "Well, I'm glad you're here, because we've got a surprise for you."

"I sure hope this works," said Abby. She wheeled the table with the traveling cage closer to the head of the bed so Elliot could reach it.

"It'll work," Elliot assured her. He unlatched the door and Chiku hopped out. "We've been practicing this for days, haven't we?"

"Practicing what?" asked Tess, still playing with Elliot's call button cord. Abby hoped she didn't accidentally summon a nurse.

"You and Chiku started off on the wrong foot," explained Elliot. "So we've been teaching her a little something special. Go on, Chiku. Say it."

Chiku preened her feathers.

"Come on, Chiku," pleaded Abby. She crossed her fingers behind her back. "You can do it."

Chiku stopped smoothing her feathers and hopped across the bed toward Tess. Abby held her breath. The parrot stared at Tess for a moment, then opened her beak.

"Silly goose!" she squawked.

"You taught her to call me a goose?" Tess cried, jumping up.

"Tess, wait," called Abby, but Tess stomped out of the room without looking back. Abby glanced helplessly at Elliot. "I have to find her before Dad gets back."

"Go," said Elliot. "I'll put Chiku back in her cage."

Abby hesitated, then raced out the door. The hallway was empty. Then she spotted the elevator doors closing.

Abby jabbed the button and slipped into another elevator as soon as it opened. She pressed the button for the fifth floor. Her stomach lurched as the elevator silently rose, then bumped to a stop a few seconds later.

Abby stepped out. This floor looked much the same as Elliot's floor, only instead of purple monkeys there were pink and blue storks on the walls. A pregnant woman in a hospital gown walked slowly toward Abby, supported by a tired-looking man. Two nurses chatted quietly and a doctor in squeaky shoes disappeared through an open doorway.

But there was no sign of Tess.

Abby was about to jump back into the elevator when the thin wail of a newborn baby floated down the hallway. She bit her lip, then sighed and let the elevator close without her. If there were babies here, Tess must be nearby.

Abby tiptoed in the direction of the crying.

"Excuse me," called one of the nurses. "Can I help you?"

Abby gulped. "No thanks," she said quickly. "I'm here for my sister."

"Just a minute," said the nurse. But Abby had already turned the corner. She thought she caught a flash of Tess's red shirt, but it was gone before she could be certain. Abby hurried forward and found herself in front of a wall with a large glass window. Behind the glass were babies. Row after row of tiny babies, each in its own little bed. Some were crying, some were sleeping, and one simply watched Abby through the glass.

Abby caught her breath. Gazing into the baby's eyes, she suddenly felt like her insides had turned to pudding. The baby was so cute and innocent, lying there…

Whoa, thought Abby, jerking her eyes away from the newborn. A few more minutes of this and I'll be as baby-crazy as the rest of my family.

Tess was hiding somewhere, she reminded herself. Dad could return to Elliot's room at any moment and if he discovered she'd left Chiku alone, her pet-sitting career would be in serious trouble. She had to do something, and fast.

Taking a deep breath, Abby reached into her pocket. She pulled out the rubber ball and held it in the air.

"Here girl!" she called, whistling sharply. "Wanna play fetch?"

Everybody on the maternity floor turned to stare.

The frowning nurse rounded the corner, heading straight for Abby. Abby's face suddenly felt hot. She swallowed hard and whistled again.

"Woof!" barked Tess, jumping out from behind a laundry cart. "Woof, woof!"

"There you are," hissed Abby. She grabbed Tess's hand and dragged her toward the elevator. "We've got to get out of here, quick."

"What about fetch?" asked Tess.

"Later," said Abby. "First we have to get back to Elliot's room before Dad does."

Abby felt a wave of relief wash over her when she pushed open Elliot's door and Dad wasn't waiting inside. Then her heart sank. Chiku's cage was empty.

And so was Elliot's bed.

15 Code Red and Gray — with a Beak!

"Not this again," groaned Tess. "We're always losing pets!"

Abby didn't answer. The fact was, she had misplaced a few animals in the past. A green anole lizard and a glow-in-the-dark hamster came to mind, but she'd never lost an entire human before!

"Where did they go?" asked Tess.

Abby shrugged her shoulders and tried to think. This pet-sitting job was a disaster! First Tess ran off, then Chiku and Elliot disappeared. Dad was never going to trust her again.

"We've got to find them," said Abby. She darted back into the hallway with Tess right behind her.

"Maybe we should split up," suggested Tess.

"No!" cried Abby. "You've done enough exploring on your own. Stick with me, Tess. We'll find them together."

They rushed down the hall, past the

nurses' station and the blue elephants. At the end of the hall Abby spied a small crowd of people, and a tingle went up her spine. She sped up. When she got there, everyone was talking at once.

"It's amazing," whispered a blonde nurse. "I can't believe it!"

"How did it happen?" asked another.

"He says he's looking for a carrot," said an elderly man in a wheelchair. He jiggled his hearing aid with a gnarled finger. "I told him the hospital food was terrible, and he should find himself a nice vending machine."

Abby pushed her way to the center of the crowd. Her mouth fell open. There, hobbling down the hallway on his crutches, was Elliot.

"What are you doing here?" cried Tess, elbowing past Abby to get a better view. "And why do you want a carrot?"

Elliot turned around to face them, teetered on the wooden crutches, then caught his balance. "Not a carrot," he said, his face pale and his eyes wide with concern. "A parrot. Chiku's missing!"

Abby's mind raced. "But how?" she demanded. "I left her with you. How could she escape?"

"The door bounced back open when you left," explained Elliot. He took a wobbly step toward Abby, then another. "I went to call a nurse with my call button, but someone had unclipped it from my pillow and it was on the floor."

Abby glared at Tess. Tess shrugged, her cheeks turning bright pink.

"I tried and tried to reach it," continued Elliot, "but my arms weren't long enough. When I looked up, Chiku was gone."

"So you used the crutches," said Abby.

Elliot looked down at the crutches with surprise. "I didn't think about it, really. I just knew I had to find Chiku. It all happened so fast."

Abby smiled. "You're walking, you know."

Elliot stared at Abby, then grinned. "I am, aren't I?"

Several of the nurses clapped. The man in the wheelchair jiggled his hearing aid until it produced a shrill, high-pitched whine. Tess was so excited she jumped up and down, nearly knocking over a stack of lunch trays.

"So where is that rude bird anyway?" she asked.

Abby and Elliot stared at each other. "We've got to find her before Dad gets back," cried Abby.

The blonde nurse shook her head. "You mean there really is a lost parrot?"

Elliot nodded. "I told you, she's gray, with a red tail."

"It couldn't have gone too far," said the nurse. She clapped her hands briskly. "Fan out, people. We're looking for a parrot. Code red . . . and gray, with a beak."

Ten minutes later, Abby was starting to panic. Dad would be back any second, and despite help from the nursing staff, they had found no sign of Chiku. Not even so much as a feather. Resigned and miserable, they headed back to Elliot's room.

Abby helped Elliot back into bed. His face was paler than usual and he sank back into the pillows with an exhausted grunt.

"I'm sorry," he said. "This is all my fault."

"No," said Abby. "It's my fault. I should have double-checked the door."

"You guys are both pretty lousy babysitters," agreed Tess. She didn't notice the dirty look Abby gave her. "When our baby comes, I'm going to put it on a leash so it can't ever run away."

"A leash?" repeated Elliot.

"Sure," said Tess. She reached into her pocket and pulled out a tattered dog leash. "This one's mine, but I'm saving my allowance to buy a brand new one for the baby. When the baby comes…"

"That's enough!" cried Abby. She slapped both hands over her ears and shook her head. "Baby, baby, baby! That's all anyone talks about anymore. I'm sick and tired of it!"

Tess stared at Abby. Her lower lip quivered. "You only care about your dumb parrot."

Abby threw her hands in the air, exasperated. "He's my client," she said. "Our client. We're on a pet-sitting job, remember? That used to be important to you. Now all you think about is the baby, and it's not even born yet."

"I love the baby, and I can't wait for it to come," said Tess, looking upset. "I'm going to be the best big sister in the whole world. Just like you."

Abby caught her breath. "Like me?" she repeated.

Tess nodded and stared back at her earnestly. Abby could feel Elliot's gaze on her too.

Abby felt ashamed. She always complained about how Tess followed her around like a little shadow she couldn't shake. Lately though, all Tess could think of was the baby. And as crazy as it sounded, Abby realized that she was feeling left out. And, deep down, she was just the tiniest bit jealous.

She thought about the newborns in the hospital nursery, and how she felt when she looked at them. It suddenly seemed silly to be resentful of something so small, so helpless.

Tess was waiting for her to speak. Abby gave her a quick hug. "Our baby is going to be the luckiest baby in the whole world," she told her. "After all, it'll have two big sisters to look out for it, right?"

16 Birdbaths and Chess Mates

"Sorry, that took longer than I thought," said Dad, stepping into the room. "I ran into Elliot's doctor and he was telling me . . ."

"I've got something to tell you, too," interrupted Abby. She had to tell Dad that she'd lost Chiku, even if it meant she would never pet-sit again. It was something she had to do. And, just like taking off a band-aid, she needed to do it fast and get it over with.

She took a deep breath. "Chiku is . . ."

Suddenly the room filled with twittering bird song. Abby whirled around to look at Elliot, but his eyes were wide with surprise. And his lips weren't moving.

"Whistling!" exclaimed Tess. "It's coming from the bathroom."

Abby ran to the small bathroom attached to Elliot's room. The door was ajar. She flung it open.

Chiku looked up at them from the sink. A drop of water formed on the end of the tap, then plopped onto her head. Chiku flapped her wings happily as the water dribbled down her back.

"Got me wellies on!" squawked Chiku. She looked at her audience and then burst into song again.

"She's having a shower," cried Abby. Tears of relief sprang to her eyes.

"I don't think the hospital would approve of her using the sink for a birdbath," said Dad. He stepped into the bathroom and held out his arm. Chiku hopped onto it. "You don't want to get in trouble with the nurses, do you?"

Abby exchanged glances with Elliot. She hid her smile as she helped put Chiku back in her cage, then locked the door. Dad pulled the chair closer to Elliot's bed and sat down.

"Elliot, I have something to tell you." He cleared his throat, then noticed the crutches leaning against the bedside table. "Did someone move your crutches?"

Elliot glanced at Abby, and shrugged. "I decided to go for a little walk today."

Dad patted Elliot's good leg. "That's wonderful!"

"Maybe I'd better try those physiotherapy exercises you've been talking about, too," said Elliot. "I think I'm kind of out of shape."

"We'll start first thing tomorrow," said Dad. He beamed at Elliot, then clapped his hand to his forehead. "Oh, I almost forgot. I wanted to tell you that I was late getting back because I ran into your doctor, Elliot. He said I could tell you the news."

Elliot stiffened. "News?"

"Good news," said Dad. "Your father has come out of his coma. He's resting now, but he's asked to see you in a little while. "

"Really?" breathed Elliot.

Dad nodded. "Yes, really."

"Woof!" yipped Tess happily. She grabbed Abby's hands and danced around the hospital room. "Woof, woof!"

When the room quieted down, Dad looked at his watch. "I guess we're just about out of time," he said.

"Oh, don't go," pleaded Elliot. "This has been the best visit. I don't want it to end yet."

"Please, Dad," begged Abby. "Just a few more minutes."

"Well," said Dad. "Your mom did say something about having steamed spinach for supper, but I suppose it wouldn't hurt to play one game of chess . . ."

"Hooray!" shouted Abby, Tess and Elliot together.

"Set up the board," grinned Dad.

Abby pulled Chiku's traveling cage closer so she could watch. The room grew quiet as Tess contemplated her first move.

"Out!" demanded Chiku.

Tess glared at her.

"Anyone for footie?" squawked Chiku.

"Shhhhh!" hissed Tess. "I'm thinking."

"Sorry spaghetti-head!" squawked Chiku. "Sorry! Sorry!"

Elliot stared at Abby. "Finally," he exclaimed, raising one hand in the air for a high five.

Abby slapped his hand and grinned. "I knew she would say it."

Then they both looked at Tess.

Tess bent close to the cage and frowned at Chiku suspiciously. "You're really sorry?"

The parrot bobbed her head and hopped forward until they were nose to beak. "Don't throw a wobbly!" she squawked.

Tess hesitated, then giggled. "Close enough. You can be on my team."

Abby and Elliot groaned.

"Don't worry," said Tess with a happy bark. "This time we'll play by Chiku's rules."

www.abbyandtess.com

Join the Abby and Tess Pet-Sitters™ Club, where you can send electronic animal postcards to your friends, write to "Dear Abby and Tess" about your pet problems, enter the Favorite Pet contest for prizes, become a "published" writer, play games and solve puzzles. Guess the secret password to get inside our tree-house headquarters!

Go to:
www.abbyandtess.com